The Magic Knitting Pattern Book

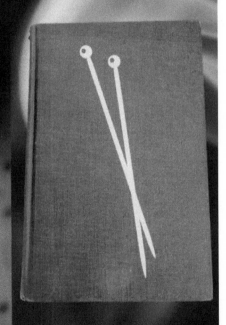

Tian Connaughton

The Magic Knitting Pattern Book

by Tian Connaughton

Thank you!

Thank you for buying this Tian Connaughton ebook.

To receive special offers, bonus content, and info on new releases, atterns, and other great reads, sign up for the newsletter.

tianconnaughton.ck.page/theweeklyyarn[1]

---

1. https://tianconnaughton.ck.page/theweeklyyarn

Copyright

CONNAUGHTON, TIAN.
The Magic Knitting Pattern Book
ISBN: 979-8-9876176-4-9 (paperback)

TO LEARN MORE ABOUT Tian Connaughton, visit www.tianconnaughton.com[3].

---

2. http://www.tianconnaughton.com

3. http://www.tianconnaughton.com

Dedication

for Daniel and Aidan

THIS BOOK WOULD NOT have been possible without the support and patience of my boys. I am forever surprised that they continue to put up with me during the long days and nights and the scraps of notes and yarn all over the house. They believed in this dream of mine. For that, I am grateful.

Chapter 1: Discovery

A sante Jones entered The Woolen Oasis dressed in her usual attire: sleek black leggings, a well-worn, oversized HBCU sweatshirt, and pink Doc Martens. The small bell above the door chimed as she walked in, she smiled at the familiar warmth of the shop. The soft tinkling announced her arrival and resonated with the shop's rich history. This cozy yarn store, nestled among charming brick buildings on bustling Main Street in the quaint small town of Sheffield Springs, served as a creative haven for knitters, crocheters, and spinners. Skeins of vibrant yarn in every hue imaginable adorned the shelves, and the walls displayed a tapestry of fiber braids from everyday sheep breeds to the most exotic. The familiar scent of wool and lanolin enveloped her, offering a comforting embrace that made her feel instantly at home.

"Hey there, Asante! Welcome! What brings you in today? On a mission to find something specific, or just soaking up the vibes of the shop?" beamed the spirited young woman, her infectious energy lighting up the already vibrant room from her spot behind the register.

"Hi, Londyn! Always a pleasure to swing by. Caught the shop's latest Youtube video showcasing the newest yarn and notions. I couldn't resist stopping in to lay eyes on the coveted ImaniJade project bags. Any chance there's a lingering bag or two in stock?" Asante beamed, her excitement palpable. She was hopeful but wasn't holding her breath. She knew ImaniJade bags vanish like magic.

"I'm sorry, Asante. We waved goodbye to the last bag yesterday. How about I pop you on the waitlist for the next wave of bags? We're expecting another batch in about six weeks, and you're on the top of the VIP list," suggested Londyn, her tone apologetic yet optimistic.

"Alright, sure. Sounds like a plan. Thanks, Londyn. While I'm here, I might as well look around and see what calls me." Asante nodded, determined to turn her quest into an adventure.

The shop's wooden floors softly creaked underfoot as Asante began her leisurely exploration. Shelves bowed under the weight of yarns, her fingers trailed along neatly stacked skeins, each a dazzling mosaic of texture and color. Cashmere's softness, merino's durability, tweed's rustic charm, and acrylic's versatility—all types of yarn, each in its place on the shelves.

As she continued her perusal, each skein was an invitation to explore. Feeling a sense of belonging amid the hum of conversations from the group knitting and crocheting around the large table, she noticed an unusual gap between some of the yarn. Hidden within this alcove, she spotted something out of place—an old, leather-bound book. Dusty and forgotten, it lay behind a stack of multicolored skeins. Asante's heart quickened. She couldn't help but reach for the book as if an invisible thread connected her, pulling her toward it, her fingertips brushing its weathered pages which held secrets woven by generations past. The book's hard cover bore the marks of time, the once embossed leather worn and aged. Its spine, ancient and weathered from decades of use, faintly displayed gilt lettering that read: 'The Magic of Knitting Patterns.'

With gentle reverence, Asante opened the book revealing yellowed pages filled with elaborate and mesmerizing knitting patterns. There were beautiful illustrations and photos of the designs, and detailed step-by-step instructions. These patterns were unlike anything she had knitted, let alone seen before. They were a testament to the artistry of generations past, each one a true masterpiece. Delicate frays at the

age edges hinted at countless knitters who had sought inspiration and
guidance within these pages.

As Asante delved deeper into the book, something even more
intriguing caught her eye. Among all the patterns, one in particular stood
out. It was a pattern for a beautiful lavender scarf. What made it unique
wasn't just its design but a note in the margins, handwritten in faded
ink, accompanying it. The note read: 'Knit this scarf to protect against
accidents.'

Asante chuckled, thinking it was some whimsical suggestion from a
long-forgotten knitter. Nonetheless, she decided it would be fun to give
the scarf pattern a try. From the vast fiber combination, she selected a soft
worsted weight merino and silk blend lavender yarn to match the image
of the design.

Asante continued to flip through the antique pattern book,
captivated, as she walked toward the counter to make her purchase. The
spot behind the register was replaced by Mrs. Anderson, the owner of
the shop. The older woman sported an intricate knitted yoke sweater, its
design and colors mimicking the vibrant essence of Kente cloth, draped
over a simple yet elegant flowing dress.

"Good day, Asante. Lyndon just dashed off for a quick break, but
he filled me in on your quest for the elusive ImaniJade project bags. I
heard the disappointment was real, but fret not—we've got your back.
We're stashing away the very first one from our upcoming order, and it's
got your name written all over it," Mrs. Anderson revealed, her assurance
echoing through the cozy shop.

"Wow, Mrs. Anderson! You're saving one for me? That's incredible.
Thank you!" she exclaimed, her excitement bubbling over.

Mrs. Anderson smiled warmly, "It's our pleasure, Dear. You're a
valuable part of our crafting community. Now, what has caught your eye
today?" she asked, eyeing the items on the counter.

"Oh, just a few things —," Asante was saying.

The bell above the door tinkled once more, announcing the arrival of another customer—an elderly woman with ornate barrel roll locs, wearing an exquisite yellow and gray brioche shawl draped over her slender shoulders. It was as if the sun had walked into the shop. She approached Asante and the shopkeeper with a friendly smile.

The older woman's eyes sparkled as she peered at the open pages of the book. "Isn't that a fascinating book?" she remarked, a wistful look filling her soft brown eyes. "I remember knitting some of those patterns when I was a young girl; they bring back such wonderful memories."

Asante couldn't help but smile in response, feeling the palpable sense of nostalgia in the air. She wondered about the stories behind those cherished memories. Out loud, she replied, "Indeed, it's a true treasure. I stumbled upon it hidden behind some yarn."

The shopkeeper, a curvy and amiable woman with graceful silver micro locs and deep, expressive brown eyes, chimed in on the conversation. "Oh, that old thing," she said, chuckling. "It's been here for ages, waiting for the right knitter to discover it. We never thought much of it, but it seems to have caught your eye."

Asante nodded. "It certainly did." Flipping to the page featuring the lavender scarf, Asante continued, "And look at this. There's a note here on this scarf pattern that says, 'Knit this scarf to protect against accidents.' It's such a peculiar instruction to include in a pattern book. Have you ever heard of such a thing? I'm intrigued by what it might mean."

The elderly woman's eyes twinkled. "Ah, that scarf," she began, her voice carrying a hint of mystery. "It's said to be a bit of a local legend around here. Some say it's just an old superstition, but others swear it has a touch of magic woven into it. I knit one for my granddaughter years ago, and she's never had a serious accident since."

Asante arched a perfectly shaped eyebrow, her curiosity piqued by the idea but tinged with a bit of skepticism. "Magic, you say?"

Mrs. Anderson shrugged. "Who knows? Knitting has its own kind of magic, bringing comfort and joy to those who create and wear the pieces. Maybe there's something to it."

As Asante paid for her yarn and the pattern book, she couldn't help but feel an overwhelming sense of curiosity and excitement. She was about to embark on a knitting project unlike any she had undertaken before, and the possibility of a little magic added an extra layer of intrigue. Little did she know that the scarf she was about to knit would not only keep her warm but also lead her on a journey filled with unexpected twists and turns.

Chapter 2: Premonition

"Time to cast on this scarf!" Asante exclaimed out loud to no one, excited to begin a new knitting project.

Nestled comfortably within her softly lit living room, Asante found herself immersed in a serene ambiance, her dark, natural hair styled in braids piled high on top of her head, wrapped in a silk scarf with a hint of an edgy blonde undercut peeking out. Beyond her windowpane, the world outside surrendered to the gentle embrace of early evening darkness. With eager anticipation tinged with a hint of unease, she embarked on her knitting journey, casting on the lavender scarf from the mysterious antique pattern book.

The scarf's pattern was elaborate and delicate, unlike any she had attempted before. It demanded careful attention to detail. Asante's fingers moved gracefully, guiding the soft yarn through each intricate twist and turn of the design. It was a slow, meticulous process of getting familiar with the stitches. Yet the rhythmic cadence of each stitch was soothing, like the gentle ebb and flow of a tranquil river.

As the evening progressed, the lavender scarf began to take shape beneath Asante's skilled hands, gradually revealing its intricate beauty. The world outside her window succumbed to the night's embrace. The steady and melodic knitting provided a comforting backdrop to her thoughts, but little did she know that the events of the next day would bring unexpected twists to her tranquil routine. Reluctantly, as the night wore on, she set the project aside and went to bed, eagerly anticipating the joy of picking it up again in the morning.

After a long day, Asante is home. The sun descended on another day casting a warm, amber glow across the room. Asante again settled back into her cozy knitting chair with her new project in hand. The lavender scarf was slowly evolving its elegant form beneath her expert guidance. While her fingers deftly wove the yarn, her mind couldn't help but revisit the intriguing note from the pattern, 'Knit this scarf to protect against accidents.' It was a suggestion both curious and whimsical, more at home in a fairy tale than reality. Yet, the memory of the recent near accident at the intersection earlier in the day lingered heavily in her mind.

Earlier that day, Asante had set out for the local art supply store, a familiar trip she had made countless times to gather some last-minute materials for her upcoming painting class. The sun had hung low on the horizon, casting long shadows across the road as she approached a bustling intersection.

Her mind had been occupied with thoughts of her next painting project when the traffic light ahead turned red. She began to slow down, preparing to stop. Just as her car came to a halt at the intersection, a speeding blue pickup truck approached from behind, seemingly undeterred by the red light. Recklessly, the truck swerved perilously around her with tires screeching in defiance of the signal, running the red light through the intersection. It came dangerously close to colliding with her car, its broken taillights searing the heart-stopping moment into her memory.

Visibly shaken, fear and adrenaline surged through her veins in that instant, and she gripped the steering wheel tightly. It was a near-miss, a fraction of a second that separated her from a potentially catastrophic accident. Her heart pounded in her chest, and the image of the speeding car stayed with her long after she had safely navigated the intersection.

The incident left her acutely aware that she had narrowly escaped a potentially life-threatening situation. As she knitted on the scarf that vening, the memory of the near accident remained vivid in her mind, aunting her thoughts.

Her fingers continued to work the delicate lace stitches of the scarf, nd with each row the pattern grew more intricate. It was challenging, to e sure, but there was an undeniable satisfaction in completing a row and onquering a new stitch pattern.

As Asante continued to knit the lavender scarf, her fingers danced ith practiced ease, navigating the complex lace stitches. The melodic lack of her needles filled the room, creating a soothing and meditative ackground noise. Nearby on the couch sat her twin sister, Aaliyah, just ight minutes her junior, a fact Asante had always taken pride in as the lder of the two. They shared the same warm, dark brown eyes, but ie sisters differed in every other way. Asante was the whimsical and nserious artist with her head always in the clouds, contrasting sharply ith Aaliyah, the pragmatic and practical lawyer with her feet firmly lanted on the ground, following in their father and grandfather's ootsteps.

Aaliyah had joined Asante for their cherished weekly Sunday dinner radition, the sisters now reveling in a glass of wine and crafting together. Vhile Asante knitted on the lavender scarf, Aaliyah crocheted on a hrift store find - a simple, partially finished ripple blanket. Amidst their onversation, Aaliyah found herself captivated by Asante's confident ands maneuvering through the cobweb-like stitches. She was filled with mix of curiosity and admiration at lavender creation unfolding before ier eyes.

Unable to contain her curiosity any longer, Aaliyah, hands never ausing their crochet work, asked, "Asante, that pattern looks incredibly omplex. Where did you find it?"

A small smile played on Asante's lips as she glanced up from her nitting. "Oh, I forgot to tell you. It's from an antique pattern book I tumbled upon at the yarn store on Main Street a few days ago. What's trange is the mysterious note about protecting against accidents. I went

into the shop for the new ImaniJade project bag and maybe a skein o
yarn for an art project for my class, and it's as if the book found me."

Intrigued, Aaliyah raised an eyebrow. "Protecting against accidents
That sounds like something out of a fairy tale or a scary movie. Do yo
really believe it?"

Pausing her knitting, Asante looked thoughtful. "I'm not sure," sh
admitted. "But after what happened at the intersection today with tha
near-miss accident, it's hard not to wonder. It was a scary situation tha
could have ended very badly. As I knit on this scarf now, I feel calm.
feel safe. It's weird to explain, but I feel like having the scarf tucked i
my purse while sitting in the passenger front seat with me protected m
today. But it could just be me projecting," she said, continuing to knit o
the scarf.

Aaliyah nodded in understanding, her gaze fixed on the lacy scar
forming in Asante's hands. "Well, I'm glad you're safe. That must hav
been very scary for you to experience," she said, her eyes refocusing o
her own project.

"Thanks, Sis!" Asante said, taking a big sip of her wine, not wantin
to meet her sister's eye. With a hint of vulnerability, she said "
sometimes wonder if I'm making the right choices. Dad and Grandp
have all been lawyers. You followed in their footsteps. I chose a path s
different from what they expected. I can't help but wonder that mayb
you all secretly wish I'd followed in their footsteps." Not daring to mee
Aaliyah's eye, she continued, "You're the good and stable sister."

"No one expected you to be a lawyer. Dad's all bark; he doesn't mea
the things he says. Deep down, he just wants us to be happy."

"I know. I just wish he approved of my career to pursue art rathe
than continue Law School and didn't give me a hard time and call me
starving artist all the time."

"He'll come around," Aaliyah encouraged. "Besides, who's th
starving artist? You have this lovely loft apartment and a fabulous caree
that takes you around the globe," she said wistfully. Changing the subjec

back to safer territory, "Now, look at this amazing scarf you're making. Even if it wasn't the scarf that protected you, you're creating something truly special, building on history. I've never seen a scarf quite like it. Who's the designer?"

Asante's fingers never stopped moving as she replied, "I don't know who the designer is," glad to be back on a safer topic. "There weren't any names or even a copyright page with information about the publisher on the inside of the book. And if there was a name on the outside cover, that has long faded. Not knowing who the designer is and the age of the patterns is what makes it so captivating. It's like knitting a piece of history, and who knows, maybe it'll bring a little extra luck into our lives." Pausing and holding up the scarf in progress to show her sister, Asante said, "The scarf doesn't look like much yet. Right now it resembles cooked spaghetti until it gets its bath and the lace is blocked out. But you can begin to see the design taking shape."

The two sisters shared a quiet moment, sipping on their favorite sweet red dessert wine, the warmth of their bond filling the cozy living room. Aaliyah finally broke the silence. "You know, maybe this scarf isn't just about luck. Maybe it's about taking control of our fate, stepping out of our comfort zone, and taking it one stitch at a time."

Asante met Aaliyah's gaze and nodded in agreement. "You might be onto something there. Perhaps there's more to this pattern than meets the eye," she said, not wanting to admit that she's been feeling stuck and unmotivated lately. She's already seen as a flighty artist and doesn't want to continue to look unreliable in front of her level-headed and consistent lawyer sister.

Aaliyah, avoiding direct eye contact, broached a sensitive topic. "Have you spoken to Dad lately?" she inquired, sensing Asante's hesitation. A tense silence hung in the air before Aaliyah persisted, concern evident in her voice. "I'm just asking because he has a doctor's appointment next week, and I'm a bit worried."

In an attempt to lighten the atmosphere and return to the carefree mood from earlier, Asante reassured her sister with a lighthearted comment. "I'm sure everything will be fine, little Sis. He's a tough old goat." The shared laughter served as a brief respite, momentarily dispelling the underlying concerns and fostering a sense of familial warmth.

Later that evening, in her quiet solitude, Asante's knitting needles continued their melodic dance. Aaliyah's words lingered at the edges of her mind like a haunting refrain in her thoughts. The lavender scarf, with its beautiful, yet complex lace stitches, transcended its role as mere fabric, morphing into a potent symbol of resilience and the remarkable capacity to forge one's own destiny. Unbeknownst to Asante, the pages of the antique pattern book held the threads of an impending journey brimming with promises of unforeseen surprises and weaving a tapestry of fate where every stitch told a tale of wonder and intrigue.

Chapter 3: Thread

Several days had passed since the unusual near-miss incident, yet it lingered on the edge of Asante's thoughts like an elusive shadow. She couldn't shake the feeling of intrigue that clung to her, intensified by the now-completed lavender scarf, which had become both a symbol of mystery and reassurance. Her yearning for the secrets concealed within the antique book had only grown stronger. Fingers itching with anticipation, she flipped through its aged pages in search of a new project. "These look great," she said to herself, eyeing a pair of blue mittens adorned with an intricate snowflake motif. This pattern, too, bore a cryptic message, 'Knit these mittens to uncover hidden truths,' written in bold block text underneath the photo of the mittens. It beckoned her, urging her to delve deeper into the enigmatic world of knitting.

Carefully selecting two colors from her extensive yarn stash—a deep, rich blue for the mitten's body and pristine white resembling freshly fallen snow for the intricate snowflake—Asante prepared to embark on another journey of creativity. The combination of colors and hard-wearing fiber content she chose showcased her knitting prowess and a keen eye for color coordination. Settling into her favorite, cozy knitting chair with a fragrant cup of herbal tea, she began casting. The mittens began with a simple ribbed pattern for the cuff and, combined with a workhorse yarn, made the project easy to start.

Hours later, as she neared the end of the ribbed cuff on the firs mitten, Asante's thoughts drifted back to the vintage pattern book sh had acquired from her local yarn store. With utmost care not to dro the cuff stitches, she set the mitten being worked on five double-pointe knitting needles aside and gently picked up the weathered tome. Its page bore the marks of history; the edges softly frayed from decades of use As she turned each page with reverence, the gentle rustling of pape provided a soothing backdrop to her contemplations. What things thi book might have seen? What experience might the knitters who mad these pieces had, she thought, reminiscing on the beginning of her ow journey with the flip of each page.

The intricate designs within the book filled her with wonder. Eacl pattern was a masterpiece, a testament to the skill and creativity o generations of knitters who had come before her. Asante couldn't hel but ponder the stories of those who had breathed life into thes patterns—their aspirations, dreams woven into their creations, and th mysteries they might have uncovered.

Who was the master knitter that created this book? Where were the now? What might have happened to them? Are they still knitting? Al these questions tickled the edges of Asante's mind, her curiosity piqued.

In this quiet moment, Asante felt an unbreakable connection to th lineage of crafters who had preceded her, an overwhelming sense of bein part of a long tradition of craftsmanship and artistry.

While she continued to knit and explore the puzzle hidden withi the antique book, the doorbell chimed, heralding Aaliyah's long-awaitec arrival for their cherished Sunday dinner. The two sisters greeted eacl other warmly with smiles and hugs before taking their places at th kitchen table. With brimming wine glasses and an array of dishes including Rice and Peas, Stew Chicken, and a fresh salad, they eagerl immersed themselves in their meal. Laughter filled the room as the exchanged the latest stories and gossip, while the previous week's episod of "Wait, Wait, Don't Tell Me!" played on the tablet and provided a cheerful backdrop to their evening.

After dinner, the sisters tidied up the kitchen and relocated to the living room, bringing the remainder of the wine with them. As they chatted and laughed, Aaliyah retrieved her current work-in-progress, an off-white crochet corner-to-corner pictograph blanket adorned with a rainbow teddy bear at the center, a gift for her pregnant paralegal's baby shower. She was cutting it pretty close to the due date but was confident the blanket would be completed before Samuel went on paternity leave. Meanwhile, Asante resumed her knitting, her fingers deftly weaving intricate patterns into the snowflake mitten. The musical clicks of her needles provided solace for her restless thoughts, captivating Aaliyah's attention.

Aaliyah watched in fascination, breaking the silence. "You're truly talented. I wish I had your knitting skills."

Asante smiled, her fingers never missing a beat. "Thank you, little Sis. But don't underestimate your own talents; you're an excellent knitter and an even better crocheter. Look at the incredible blanket you're making. That's one lucky baby. I can't even crochet!"

Aaliyah chuckled. "True, you can't crochet to save your life!"

Both sisters shared a light-hearted moment before returning to their crafting and their own thoughts. Asante's mind, however, remained fixated on the antique pattern book and the mysteries it held. She couldn't help but ponder the people who had used these patterns in the past, their untold stories, and the connections that bound them to this ancient volume. Out loud she asked, "Do you ever wonder about the people who might have knitted and crocheted from pattern books before us?"

Aaliyah, her gaze drifting to the antique pattern book on the coffee table opened to the mitten patterns, mused, "Who knows? Perhaps they were artists like us, seeking inspiration from the past, an escape from the present, or they were simply ordinary individuals finding peace in creating something beautiful like us. What do you think?"

With newfound determination gleaming in her eyes, Asante replied "You're absolutely right. There's something about this book, a connection to the past that we can't ignore between the people who knit the patterns and the designers who created them. I'm not entirely sure what it is, but I'm drawn to it like an invisible thread has me tethered. I'm resolved to uncover the mysteries of what these cryptic messages might mean, one pattern at a time."

Aaliyah offered her warm support. "I don't doubt that you'll uncover this mystery. You've always achieved everything you set out to do. Please keep me updated and let me know how I can help."

As the sisters exchanged thoughts and ideas, the background podcast continued to play, providing a comforting ambiance. Suddenly, the tablet chimed, and a breaking news headline alert flashed across the tablet's screen, capturing Asante's attention. Recent events piqued her curiosity, and she quickly opened the news story.

On the screen, a news anchor delivered a follow-up report on the developing story of a high-profile art burglary that had occurred the previous night, casting a shadow of intrigue over their cozy evening.

The stolen artwork was a masterpiece created by a renowned Benin artist, Kofi, celebrated for his vibrant and evocative works. What made this particular piece unique was its depiction of a world the artist had never physically experienced—the beauty of fresh snowfall. The painting featured a captivating scene of a child no older than six years old, wearing a blue mitten adorned with delicate white snowflakes, reflecting the artist's fascination with a climate so different from his own. Among the series, the stolen painting was the most prized piece.

The news report displayed images of the stolen painting, a breathtaking masterpiece that seemed to encapsulate the essence of winter with every brushstroke. The art world was in uproar over the udacious theft, and the police were diligently working to recover the valuable artwork.

Overcome with emotion, Asante's fingers fumbled as she eagerly flipped the pages of the pattern book to the image of the mitten she was knitting on and held it up for Aaliyah to see. She couldn't contain the rush of elation and uncertainty that surged through her. Her heart raced, and a sense of wonder mingled with a hint of unease.

"Look!" Asante exclaimed, her voice trembling with excitement and disbelief. "The mitten in the painting is identical to the one I'm knitting on from this book."

Setting her blanket aside, Aaliyah moved closer to her sister as if in a trance. She took the book and carefully examined the mittens on the page, comparing them to those on the tablet screen. "You're right. They are identical. How interesting! What does it mean, do you think?"

Wide-eyed, Asante shrugged.

The story of the painting and artist captivated Asante's heart. Watching the news unfold, she felt a deep connection to the artist's fascination with snow in a world far from his own; his ability to accurately capture something so foreign that he'd never personally experienced. The theft of his masterpiece was a tale that stirred her imagination. "How did he arrive at this image so clearly?" she mused.

The news report continued. Asante's thoughts swirled with empathy for Kofi. As a professional artist herself, she knew the profound bond artists had with their work. The stolen painting, with its depiction of a world so different from Kofi's own, resonated with her artistic soul of being able to capture an imagination on canvas, and the mittens with her knitting experience of bringing someone else's imaginings to life. It felt like a piece of her own heart had been taken. The theft of his masterwork was a tale that not only stirred her imagination but struck a deep chord within her as an artist. She couldn't help but ponder the sacrifices and passion that went into the creation of such a gem, only for it to be snatched away.

Asante took a deep breath, her eyes briefly closed, allowing the weight of the news to settle in. At that moment, she felt an overwhelming connection to the stolen painting, the artist who had captured the beauty of a distant world, and the mysterious book in her hands. What does it all mean? She thought for the hundredth time. Her emotions swirled, a mixture of empathy for the artist, wonder at the uncanny resemblance, and a growing sense of responsibility to uncover the truth behind it all. She picked up her knitting again, the familiar weight of the needles and fabric a comfort.

Together, Asante and Aaliyah continued to watch the news report with bated breath. The story had taken an unexpected turn, and a police officer was now being interviewed.

Officer Jenkins, a seasoned detective, known for his sharp eye and no-nonsense demeanor, dressed in a dark and well-worn suit, stood in front of a crowd on the steps of the gallery where the painting had been stolen. His stern expression conveyed the urgency of the case. "We are determined to recover this artwork," he declared, his deep voice brimming with commitment. "Not just because of its monetary value but its cultural significance. It's a masterpiece that tells a unique story, and we won't rest until we bring it back to where it belongs."

Asante and Aaliyah exchanged glances, their hearts heavy with the gravity of the situation. This isn't the type of thing that happens in their sleepy little town. The officer's words resonated with Asante, mirroring her own determination to unravel the mysteries surrounding the antique pattern book and its connection to the stolen painting.

Unable to tear her eyes away from the screen, Asante leaned closer to Aaliyah and whispered, "Did you hear that? The stolen painting—it's more than just a valuable piece of art. It's a story waiting to be told."

Aaliyah nodded, her curiosity ignited. "And perhaps, somehow, that story is linked to your antique pattern book and those mittens."

With a sparkle of excitement in her eyes, Asante continued to knit, her fingers moving with practiced grace. "I have a feeling we're on the

rink of discovering something extraordinary, Aaliyah. Something that
ill weave together these mysteries in ways we could never have
nagined."

As she continued to knit, Asante couldn't shake the feeling that the
ysteries surrounding the antique pattern book and the stolen painting
ere intricately intertwined. But how? It was a thought that set the
age for an exploration into the unknown, where threads of destiny and
eativity would weave a tapestry of intrigue.

Chapter 4: Unravel

Asante's relentless curiosity propelled her deeper into the puzzling history of the antique pattern book. The cryptic notes within its pages 'Knit this scarf to protect against accidents' and 'Knit these mittens to uncover hidden truths' had transformed from a mere oddity into a tantalizing portal to a world beyond the ordinary.

Her quest for knowledge began in the dark confines of her local library basement, where she dedicated hours to immersing herself in old newspapers, dusty archives, and musty records. Amidst the dimly lit aisles, she unearthed traces of the antique pattern book in the old files, indicating its origins stretching back decades. However, the most riveting revelation emerged in the form of a faded newspaper article from the late 1900s—one that introduced her to the captivating figure of Elizabeth "Bessie" Washington, a local craftswoman.

After hours of further research, Asante had collected a wealth of information about Bessie and her legendary knitting. The tales of psychic scarves, truth-revealing mittens, and guidance-giving socks had ignited her curiosity and filled her with wonder. As she organized her notes and records in the dimly lit corner of the library basement, an old diary caught her attention.

From the writing, it appeared that the diary belonged to a mysterious figure from the past, someone who had been close to Bessie. It was unclear who this special person was, however, the diary's pages contained cryptic entries that hinted at a hidden knitting circle and mystifying rituals. Phrases like 'the guardians of the yarn' and 'the thread that binds the past and the present' sent a shiver down Asante's spine.

She couldn't shake the feeling that this diary held the key to deeper secrets. There was a darkness to the stories, a mystery that seemed far from over. Asante couldn't help but think that her journey was about to take an even more unexpected turn, and she was both thrilled and apprehensive about what she might uncover next.

Intrigued by her findings, Asante couldn't resist the urge to share her discoveries with someone who understood her relentless pursuit of the book's mysteries. With a sense of excitement building within her, she dialed Aaliyah's number, eager to reveal the secrets she had unveiled.

Bessie had been a master knitter and had gained local fame for her intricate patterns and, more notably, her reputation as a psychic knitter. Stories abounded of Bessie's uncanny ability to infuse her patterns with guidance and foresight.

Aaliyah answered the phone, and before she could utter a greeting, Asante leapt in, brimming with enthusiasm to share her findings. "Hold on to your yarn, Aaliyah! You won't believe what I've unraveled so far," she exclaimed. "Bessie, the brilliant mind behind the antique pattern book, was no ordinary designer. She's said to have knitted scarves that protected travelers, mittens that revealed hidden truths, and socks that guided wearers through personal challenges. It's like she was a psychic possessing mystical foresight, and her needles were weaving magic into every stitch."

"A psychic knitter? Like Miss Cleo from the 90's infomercials? And a secret knitting circle? That just sounds so silly," Aaliyah giggled from the other end of the phone.

"I don't know," Asante answered. "I believe it." A bit hurt by her sister's quick dismissal.

"Oh, sure, Sis!"

There was a long awkward pause.

"Oh, you're serious! I'm sorry. I was only joking." Aaliyah apologized sincerely. Not wanting to discourage or dismiss her sister's findings, she continued, "Tell me more."

"Thanks for apologizing." Changing the subject away from her lightly hurt feelings, Asante continued to share more about the information she'd discovered so far about Bessie and her designs. I haven't been able to locate any information about the pattern book, who published it, or anything.

"Maybe it was self-published," Aaliyah suggested.

"That's what I thought too but it's so professionally bound, with really great photos and illustrations. That makes me think it was done by a publishing house, but I don't know. I don't even know for sure if Bessie is the designer here," Asante said.

Asante was captivated by Bessie's story. The thought that the antique pattern book might be linked to this legendary knitter filled her with excitement and wonder. "Maybe she was an obeah woman, infusing her magic into her knitting? I'm stuck on what to do next. I'm at a loss," she whined to Aaliyah. "I'm an artist, not a researcher," she sighed.

"Take a deep breath. You don't have to know every step to take right now, just figure out the very next thing to do and go from there," Aaliyah soothed. "Continue to research the files you've found in the archives. Talk to people. Bessie was a local. Maybe go to the Council on Aging to see if anyone there knew her. Go back to the yarn store and see what they might know about her designs."

Asante gave a huge sigh, grateful for her sister's level head and ability to reason through a problem. "Thanks, Sis. Those are great suggestions. You always know how to get me back on track when I lose focus and get overwhelmed."

The call ended. Feeling clearer about her next steps, Asante continued her research, scouring historical records. She contacted the director of the Council on Aging about talking to elderly town residents who might have known Bessie or heard stories about her extraordinary knitting abilities.

Still sitting in the archives with the antique pattern book open in front of her, Asante pulled out her current work in progress from her purse. Her fingers hesitated over the knitting needles as she remembered the scarf her grandmother had made for her so long ago before passing away. This scarf had always brought her comfort, and she couldn't help but feel a connection between her own passion for knitting and her grandmother's love. Her warm smile and the way she would wrap the scarf around Asante's neck before sending her off to play in freshly fallen snow flooded her thoughts.

Asante's eyes welled up with tears, and she realized that her quest for Bessie Washington's secrets was more than just idle curiosity. It was a way to honor her grandmother's memory and the craft that had brought them so much joy. She whispered a promise to her grandmother's memory, "I'll find the truth, and I'll make you proud."

A few days later, on a sunny afternoon, Asante gathered her findings and headed to the yarn store where she had discovered the antique book. The store, with its rustic charm and welcoming atmosphere, was bustling with customers and knitting enthusiasts. The gentle hum of conversation filled the air as customers examined skeins of yarn, comparing colors and textures.

Asante approached Mrs. Anderson seated among a group of knitters and crocheters. She was at the large table near the back of the shop crocheting on a lacy shawl with an allover pineapple stitch pattern. Asante waited until Mrs. Anderson was at the end of the row and made a note on the pattern before jumping in. With enthusiasm, Asante shared her discoveries about the antique pattern book she purchased, the designer being Bessie Washington, and her legendary psychic knitting abilities. The customers who overheard her conversation gathered around the table, their interest piqued.

Asante recounted Bessie's story from her research and conversations with senior citizens who knew her and could confirm that she was the designer of the pattern book. She could see the fascination in the eyes of those listening. They marveled at the idea that knitting could be more than just a craft; it could be a conduit for magic, spirituality, and guidance.

Amid the conversation, Mrs. Anderson recommended, "You know, dear, if you're truly interested in learning more about Bessie Washington and her legacy, there's someone you should meet. LaShawn Davie, our local historian, is a regular at our Sunday Brunch n' Stitch gatherings here at the store. They are not only passionate about knitting but also a treasure trove of historical knowledge on the topic. I'm sure they would be eager to help you unravel the threads of this mystery."

With a sense of excitement, Asante agreed to meet LaShawn during the next upcoming Sunday Brunch n' Stitch session at The Woolen Oasis, eager to delve deeper into the mysterious history of the antique pattern book and the designer. It was a meeting that would set the stage for a partnership and friendship that would uncover the secrets of Bessie Washington's legacy and the magic of knitting.

ASANTE'S EXCITEMENT was palpable as she prepared to meet LaShawn at the yarn store for the Sunday Brunch n' Stitch session. She arrived with Aaliyah in tow at the cozy yarn store well before the scheduled time, her heart brimming with expectation. The store, bathed in the soft, golden glow of pendant lights hanging from exposed wooden beams, hummed with the gentle chatter of knitters and crocheters, the rhythmic whirl of the spinning wheels, and the faint scent of freshly brewed tea, fresh pastries, and tropical fruits. It felt like a welcoming haven of creativity and community, each skein of yarn on the shelves holding the promise of a new project and each smiling face a potential friend.

Aaliyah, the social butterfly, immediately went off to explore th spinning wheels and vibrant colors of spinning fibers available to pla with. Asante, the introvert and wallflower, settled into a quiet corne with her knitting project, nearing the end of the second of the blu mittens with white snowflakes. Asante couldn't help but strike up conversation with the woman sitting next to her, an older knitter name Beatrice, who was also knitting mittens, for her grandson.

Recognizing the mitten pattern that Asante was knitting on Beatrice had a mischievous glint in her eye as she said, "Ah, so you're th one digging into Bessie Washington's mysteries, aren't you?"

Asante nodded eagerly. "Yes, that's me. I'm fascinated by her stor and the possibilities it holds. Did you know her?"

Beatrice chuckled softly, her knitting needles clicking away. "Well I'm not that old," she giggled. "My grandmother used to tell me storie about Bessie when I was just a little girl. She said that Bessie's knittin needles sang when she worked on a special project. It was as if the yar itself whispered secrets to her."

Asante's eyes widened with intrigue. "That sounds amazing. Do yo think there's any truth to those tales?"

Beatrice leaned in closer, her voice lowered conspiratorially. "Well my grandmother swore that the scarf Bessie knitted for her brought he good luck throughout her life. She said it was more than just yarn and stitches; it was a guardian of sorts. There were also a lot of whispers abou the mystical knitting circle she held every week at her house. I remembe hearing wild stories about those meetups."

Before Asante could inquire further, a friendly voice interruptec their conversation. "I couldn't help but overhear your discussion," said person with a warm smile, long locs cascading over their shoulders, and defined chiseled features. Sitting down, their knitting needles dancec in their hands. "I'm LaShawn, the local historian Mrs. Anderson mentioned. I've been researching Bessie's legacy for years, and I have few stories of my own to share."

Asante's heart skipped a beat as she greeted LaShawn, feeling the magic of the moment. The store's ambiance seemed to shimmer with the promise of unraveling secrets and uncovering the mystical world of knitting.

"Hi. I'm Asante," she said shyly, offering her hand to LaShawn to shake. "And that is my sister, Aaliyah, over there playing on the spinning wheel," she continued with a nod in her sister's direction, her eyes never leaving LaShawn's perfectly symmetrical face.

With a twinkle in their eye, LaShawn began to speak, "You see, Bessie Washington's knitting held more than just warmth and practicality. It wasn't just knitting, like we know it. It held the power of connection, of understanding the world in a different way. Her patterns were like maps to the human heart, and her needles, well, they were the keys to unlocking its mysteries. Some said she possessed magical powers, an obeah woman, stemming from her African and Caribbean roots."

As the afternoon wore on, Asante, Beatrice, and LaShawn shared stories of Bessie's remarkable creations, each one imbued with its own unique magic. The gathering of stitchers and spinners listened in rapt attention, their hands busy with their own projects, their imaginations sparked by the tales of psychic scarves, truth-revealing mittens, and guidance-giving socks.

Asante looked around and smiled, realizing that she was not alone in her quest to uncover the secrets of the antique pattern book and Bessie Washington's legacy. In this cozy corner of the world, amidst the click of needles and the warmth of friendship, she felt like she was on the brink of an extraordinary adventure—one that would knit together the past and the present in ways she could never have imagined.

Chapter 5: Friendship

S unday Brunch n' Stitch at The Woolen Oasis continued. A delightful gathering of individuals from diverse backgrounds, all united by their shared love for yarn and fiber. Among the eclectic mix, a unique partnership had blossomed between Asante, an accomplished artist, and LaShawn, a local historian known for their skill in unraveling the mysteries of the past. Their connection seemed almost fated, a harmonious blend of creativity and scholarship guided by the mystic antique pattern book.

Away from the hum of other stitchers and spinners, Asante and LaShawn found a quiet nook in the yarn store. Nestled in their cozy corner, they dove into animated conversation about the intricate lace sock pattern from the antique pattern book they had chosen for their joint knitting venture. Opting for the recommended worsted weight yarn signaled a departure for Asante, accustomed to the delicate nature of knitted socks worked in fingering weight yarn.

The design, a masterpiece attributed to the skilled hands of Bessie Washington, unraveled a tale of unparalleled craftsmanship. Delicate lacework wove a narrative with every precisely executed stitch. Exquisite textures adorned the surface of the socks, reminiscent of vintage charm. As they delved into the project, the yarn store became a cocoon where tradition and creativity intersected, threading together a story as enchanting as the socks taking shape beneath their fingertips.

The socks within the pages of the book unfolded in a harmonious blend of natural, undyed tones, casting a spell of nostalgia and authenticity. A closer gaze revealed that the lace patterns were not mere decorative embellishments; they harbored a deeper hidden significance. Each stitch seemed to morph into cryptic symbols, akin to a secret message waiting to be unraveled. The overall effect was nothing short of enchanting, as if the twist of the pattern held the whispered secrets of a story untold, beckoning Asante and LaShawn to embark on the quest for revelation. A moment of profound silence enveloped them, each lost in thoughts that oscillated between the intricacies of the pattern, their yarn choices, and the deeper meaning woven into its creation.

Breaking the tranquil silence, Asante, her gaze locked on her knitting, spoke first. "LaShawn," she said with a hitch of hesitation in her voice. "Have you ever encountered lacework of such intricacy? The socks appear to be ordinary at first glance, but you can tell they hold within them the promise of hidden knowledge and a connection to Bessie's family history and psychic abilities. It's as though Bessie poured her very essence into the fabric of every stitch."

LaShawn nodded, their fingers moving gracefully over their needles. "I've knitted advanced sock patterns before, but the level of complexity and precision in this pattern speaks volumes about Bessie's talents, dedication, and artistry. I can't help but wonder what inspired her to craft such exquisite beauty. Unlike the scarf, this pattern doesn't give a warning, but there is something there. There is a story."

As their hands moved in perfect synchrony, their knitting needles produced a harmonious melody, infusing life into Bessie's pattern. With each intricate stitch, Asante and LaShawn felt a profound connection to the legendary knitter, as if they were weaving the threads of her life into the fabric of their friendship.

Amidst the rhythmic clicking of their needles, they delved deeper into Bessie's life, each sharing what they'd gathered so far. LaShawn's access to historical records and databases as a researcher provided

ntalizing glimpses into the past, revealing that Bessie had been born
the very town they now called home—a discovery that added an
triguing layer to her enigmatic story.

Pausing for a moment, Asante's eyes sparkled with curiosity. "Can
u imagine what it must have been like for Bessie, growing up in this
wn and honing her craft? I bet she had some interesting experiences
d an array of incredible stories to share."

LaShawn smiled warmly. "I'm certain she did. And we are fortunate
 have the opportunity to unearth those stories, one stitch at a time.
ut I do wonder why all these treasures are in dusty basement libraries
nd not with her family. Shouldn't they have all these memories of her
gacy?"

"I wondered the same thing too when I first discovered the pattern
ook and learned who the author was. This was something I asked about
 the Council on Aging and was told that she didn't have any family left.
fter she died, her estate was sold off and her belongings were scattered
round the county." Asante was saddened to learn this from the elders
e spoke to. Bessie had created so much while she was alive. Asante
anted to make sure her story lived on.

"How sad?" They both agreed. They both fell into a weighted silence
 each retreated to their own thoughts about what the final days of
essie's life might have been like.

As the hour grew late, and Aaliyah lingered by the notions near
he register, Asante sensed it was time to leave. Despite having known
aShawn for just a few hours, it felt like a connection spanning much
nger.

"We should get going," Asante said, nodding towards her sister. "I'll
xt you and we can make a date—," Asante stammered, her face flushed
ith warmth at the suggestion of a date. Clearing her throat, she said, "I
ean to say, we can make a plan to do more research together."

With a smile, LaShawn agreed, and they exchanged numbers. Asante
alked away, unable to resist stealing a glance back.

"You look a bit flushed. What happened back there?" Aaliyah asked. She glanced at LaShawn and chuckled. "Never mind. I can see," she teased. The sisters exited the store and headed back to Asante's apartment for their weekly Sunday dinner together.

The following day, Asante was still buzzing with the contagious energy she'd experienced from her initial encounter with LaShawn. They had agreed to partner up to find out more about Bessie. Their research became a journey through time and knowledge, leading them to dusty archives on the university campus where LaShawn worked. Here, ancient manuscripts and forgotten narratives whispered secrets of Bessie's past. The duo also delved into the rich memories of elderly town residents. The interviews uncovered cherished stories that painted a vivid image of the enigmatic Bessie.

They learned that in her later years, Bessie had become somewhat of a recluse, rarely seen outside her quaint home. Whispers about her psychic abilities had circulated through the town for decades, with some claiming she could predict the weather and exact birth times of babies with uncanny accuracy.

In their unwavering pursuit of the truth, Asante and LaShawn stumbled upon old journals and handwritten letters that confirmed Bessie's profound connection to the antique pattern book. She had frequently written about her "magical" patterns and how they had been guiding lights through the storms of life.

Amidst the faded ink, Asante's eyes caught a peculiar diary entry about knitting socks for a woman to give to her abusive husband. Bessie wrote about "cleansing" the socks as part of the finishing process. Remarkably, once the husband received the socks, which he'd worn every day, he completely changed. The once abusive partner became the loving and attentive husband the woman needed.

"This goes beyond the usual washing and blocking of finished socks. It feels like a ritual," Asante mused to herself. Her eyes widened with excitement as she couldn't contain her discovery. "LaShawn, it's as if hese patterns were Bessie's companions, her confidants throughout her ife. I can't shake the feeling that there's more to them than simply nstructions to recreate a piece of knitting. Something deeper is waiting o be uncovered."

"Look at this note," LaShawn pointed to a yellowed page in an old liary they were reading. "It's hard to read because the ink is so faded with ge, but that," they pointed to a bit of writing in the middle of the page, looks like a knit stitch symbol. It's written in cursive, which I have a hard ime deciphering, but I believe those are symbols for knit stitches. It's like language of its own."

"You're right. It looks like knitting. But do those words there," Asante said, pointing to the sentence below, "do they say 'blood' and snow'? I can't make out the writing clearly. Maybe someone at the Council on Aging can help us translate the parts that aren't too faded."

The room buzzed with excitement. Clues surfaced, similar to concealed stitches in a complex lace pattern—evidence woven into the rich tapestry of Bessie's extraordinary life. But what did it all mean? It felt ike it was all leading somewhere, but the instructions were unclear.

As they continued to knit and unveil the well-guarded secrets of Bessie's past, Asante and LaShawn forged a friendship that transcended their differences. They shared stories of personal challenges and dreams, finding solace in the meditative rhythm of their knitting and the echoes of Bessie's intriguing history.

Filled with warmth, Asante remarked, her eyes reflecting a deep sense of gratitude, "I never anticipated that knitting would lead me to such an extraordinary friendship. You're not just my knitting partner; you're my partner in exploration. The threads we weave together with every stitch of this sock seem to mirror the bonds we're creating in our quest to uncover the mysteries of Bessie's world. It's a journey I wouldn't trade for anything else."

LaShawn nodded, their eyes reflecting the sentiment. They leaned in slightly, their voice carrying a subtle undercurrent of something more profound. "And you've added a new dimension to my historical research I never imagined history could be so beautifully intertwined with creativity. It's not just the past we're uncovering; it's a future of endless possibilities that we're weaving together with every discovery and every shared moment, Asante."

With each stitch, Asante and LaShawn delved deeper into the intricate web of Bessie Washington's legacy, unraveling the mysteries of her life and the extraordinary world she had inhabited. As they revealed the well-hidden secrets of the past, they couldn't help but wonder what other surprises the antique pattern book held and how it might continue to guide them on their extraordinary journey of friendship and discovery.

ONE QUIET AFTERNOON, as they sat engrossed in their research in the university library basement, the air around them filled with the hushed rustling of diaries they had unearthed from Bessie's personal archives. Asante paused and turned her gaze to LaShawn, her eyes alight with a thoughtful glimmer. Leaning in closer to whisper, she couldn't contain her excitement. "You know, LaShawn, there's something I've been avidly following in the news and newspapers," she began, the words tinged with an air of shared anticipation. "It's about a rather unusual incident—a daring heist of a renowned painting from the local art gallery."

LaShawn's eyes widened in intrigue. They didn't spend too much time in the art world but were more than content to just listen as Asante spoke. Sensing Asante's excitement, they leaned in closer too. "A heist? Tell me more," they urged, their interest piqued.

Asante picked up her knitting, her nimble fingers worked the now-familiar intricate lace pattern with practiced ease. Unbeknownst to her, that very sock pattern would soon intertwine a new and unexpected twist. She relayed the thrilling tale of the painting heist to LaShawn, haring the details she had gathered from news reports and articles. Her yes sparkled with excitement as she wove the story seamlessly into the abric of their conversation, each word drawing LaShawn further into he captivating narrative. She couldn't help but feel a curious shiver down ier spine as her knitting needles moved. Her fascination with the painting heist, a story she'd been following closely, was about to become in integral part of her journey.

The dim lighting of the room seemed to dance in rhythm with Asante's animated gestures, casting playful shadows on her face and causing her eyes to sparkle. At that moment, the ordinary became extraordinary. The threads of their friendship and the mysteries of the antique book intertwined with the intrigue of the stolen painting, creating a rich tapestry of shared discoveries and whispered secrets. Within the cozy confines of the library archives grew the promise of adventure and the anticipation of uncovering secrets beyond their wildest dreams.

What did the heist have to do with Bessie? It was all connected somehow. As Asante and LaShawn immersed themselves further into Bessie's enchanted world, they couldn't shake the feeling that the stolen painting might be intricately linked to the mystical symbols in Bessie's patterns, as if each stolen brushstroke mirrored the secret language woven into her knitted creations.

Chapter 6: Mystery

The next evening, Asante nestled into her cherished armchair, the worn cushions embracing her like an old friend. The soft lamplight anced off the intricate stitches of the pattern as she diligently worked n the heel of the second sock. In the past, second sock syndrome had lagued her, like a relentless riddle she couldn't solve. Yet, tonight, the eedles moved with a newfound ease, as if the very pattern whispered ecrets only she could understand.

As the yarn wound through her fingers, Asante's mind unraveled he strands of the mystery surrounding the stolen painting and Bessie's ntique book. The connection fascinated her, an invisible thread linking wo seemingly unrelated worlds. An idea took shape in her mind, akin o knitting, that resembled cooked spaghetti magically transforming into eautiful lace after blocking. Setting aside her knitting needles, letermination etched across her face, she decided it was time to weave er own narrative into the unfolding mystery.

With the click-clack of the needles now silent, Asante reached for er phone, the sleek device a portal to collaboration. Dialing LaShawn's umber, she felt a flutter of excitement in her chest. The phone rang n the other end, each ring echoing like a heartbeat in the quiet room. When LaShawn's voice filled the line, Asante wasted no time, "There as to be a connection between the stolen painting and Bessie's antique ook. How about we go check out the gallery and see if there are any clues?" The transition from solitude to shared purpose was seamless, much like the stitches in the socks she crafted with care.

"Hi, Asante. How are you? It's so nice to hear from you," LaShawn' warm voice greeted her.

"Oh, sorry. You know how I get. My mind is moving at lightspeed."

"I do. Now, what were you saying about the gallery?" LaShawn asked, curiosity tingling their words.

"We should go to the gallery to search for clues. I can pretend to inquire about an art showing. That would be a perfect way to ask questions without drawing suspicion."

"You sure about this, Asante? I, too, want to see how the puzzle pieces all fit together—if they even fit at all—but shouldn't we leave this to the cops to solve? This could be dangerous. They don't teach crime-solving at historian college." LaShawn's hesitation to play sleuth battled with wanting to do whatever was possible to be in Asante' company.

Asante grinned; her voice filled with mischief. "Oh, come on LaShawn. Where's your sense of adventure?"

"It's been a wild adventure since the day we met at the Sunday Brunch n' Stitch," LaShawn said wryly.

"Noted," Asante replied with a little giggle. "We'll be careful and turn over whatever information we gather to the detective working the heist case," crossing her heart with a mock salute, "promise!"

LaShawn couldn't help but grin. "Alright, Detective Asante, but I still don't like it," they replied with a playful tone.

"Great. See you tomorrow."

THE QUAINT TOWN, NESTLED in the soft embrace of a chilly autumn afternoon, hummed with a quiet vibrancy as Asante and LaShawn embarked on their quest. Their journey had brought them to the doorstep of Enchanted Art Gallery. Here, amidst the rustling leaves nd the crisp breeze, they stood before the grand entrance, a historic building adorned with ivy-covered walls and intricate wrought-iron details. The gallery exuded an air of sophistication and artistic charm that seemed to blend seamlessly with the natural beauty of the season. Its large windows framed captivating glimpses of nature's beauty outside.

As Asante and LaShawn entered the art gallery, the weight of the mystery bore down on them. The air pulsed with the scent of aged canvases and the subtle undertones of turpentine. Asante's excitement shimmered in her eyes, but beneath it, a flicker of uncertainty hinted at the gravity of their investigation. LaShawn's hesitation was more than just caution—it was a blend of fear and loyalty, a complexity that played out in the subtle twists of their expression.

Their eager anticipation heightened as they stepped through the entrance into the captivating space. The walls were canvases themselves, adorned with meticulously curated paintings that spanned various styles and eras. Each stroke of the artist's brush whispered to the passage of time and to the gallery's commitment to showcasing the finest works of art. A cascade of colors unfolded before them, from the ethereal blues that captured the essence of a tranquil sky to the fiery reds that seemed to dance with the flicker of an unseen flame.

Mrs. Fitzgerald welcomed them to the gallery with a bright and vibrant smile, a stark contrast to her formal attire finished with a severe bun at the nape of her neck. Her knowledge of art and keen eye for beauty matched the brilliance of the colors that graced the canvases lining the walls.

They strolled through the gallery. Each painting seemed to be more than just art; they were windows to another world, filled with emotion and history. Kofi's strokes spoke volumes, and his colors danced with passion. With each step, they ventured deeper into the gallery's enchanting embrace, the visual tapestry of emotions and mysteries unraveling before their eyes.

Mrs. Fitzgerald, a wellspring of information about the gallery's exhibits, enthusiastically shared intriguing details about the origins and interpretations of some of the paintings. At the end of the expansive main floor hall, their attention was captured by a masterpiece by Kofi, a Beninese artist. The title, "Child Two Wearing Blue Mittens with White Snowflakes" beckoned them closer. The canvas depicted a child wearing a blue mitten, each delicate snowflake hand-painted with a precision that bordered on the divine. The vivid portrayal struck a chord, echoing the haunting beauty of Bessie's legendary mitten knitting patterns. While distinct from the stolen painting, this masterpiece clearly belonged to the same gripping series.

As they examined the piece, it was impossible not to feel the chill in the air, as though winter itself had been captured on canvas. The play of light and shadow added a dynamic quality to the painting, casting an ever-changing glow that mirrored the uncertainty of their investigation. The gallery, once a sanctuary of art, now seemed like a portal to a realm where the boundaries between reality and imagination blurred.

"These are all so lovely. What about that one with the child wearing blue mittens?" LaShawn asked, pointing to what they had correctly guessed to belong to Kofi.

Mrs. Fitzgerald explained the backstory of the piece, her voice a blend of artistic intrigue and mystery. "Kofi's inspiration for this masterpiece emerged from tales of snow shared by a friend who had ventured into colder climates. Fueled by these stories and guided by visions induced through rigorous fasting and the use of herbs, he painstakingly captured the very essence of winter. The artist recounted receiving visions—one that featured an old woman knitting those exact mittens, surrounded by other women in a circle of communal creation. He confessed to not fully grasping the meaning but felt compelled to immortalize it on canvas."

This revelation presented a captivating juxtaposition—an artist who had never encountered snow, yet skillfully crafted a scene that closely echoed Bessie's design fascination with a world so different from her own.

Mrs. Fitzgerald, with an air of refined sophistication, led them to her office, pausing often to point out a new acquisition or a piece of particular interest. Approaching an empty frame, Mrs. Fitzgerald indicated that was where the stolen painting had once hung. The vacant display seemed like an eerie void, a painful reminder of the theft that had rocked the art community.

As they reached the unoccupied frame, Asante paused briefly to examine the signature, her discerning eye caught the faint etchings on the wooden surface. Her excitement radiated in her voice as she whispered to LaShawn, her words trembling with anticipation. "This is it," she breathed. "These etchings...they mirror the patterns in the book. It's like a code."

LaShawn, equally captivated by the discovery, nodded in agreement as they proceeded to the office. "It's all interconnected, Asante. The book, the patterns, Kofi's visions...it's as though they carry a message from the past, transcending time." LaShawn whispered.

Observing their exchange with both curiosity and concern, Mrs. Fitzgerald couldn't help but inquire, "What are you two discussing? This is highly irregular, to say the least."

With a measured tone, Asante replied, "We're just so intrigued by the frame. It's a piece of art in itself, much like the painting it once held. May I take a closer look?"

Mrs. Fitzgerald hesitated for a moment, then spoke with a hint of sadness. "Of course. We are devastated by the theft of this piece. It was truly priceless."

LaShawn interjected, their curiosity piqued. "But not so priceless that it wasn't insured, right? It must have been insured for a substantial amount."

Mrs. Fitzgerald sighed, admitting, "Well, yes, all the pieces in the gallery are fully insured. So, if you decide to collaborate, your work will be safe."

Asante, pretending to admire the frame, turned it around and spotted the names 'Harriet' and 'Elizabeth' discreetly carved into the corners on the back. Her heart raced as she replaced the frame, and in an attempt to deflect attention, she stated a bit too loudly, "We should continue."

Mrs. Fitzgerald's office within the gallery exuded an aura of curated elegance. The walls adorned with tasteful artwork created a harmonious backdrop to the room. A mahogany desk, a centerpiece of authority, stood near a large window allowing filtered sunlight to gently illuminate the space. As Asante and LaShawn entered, Mrs. Fitzgerald, a paragon of refined composure, slipped as she rushed to her desk. Among a cascade of papers meticulously arranged on her desk, one with red lettering caught LaShawn's eye before Mrs. Fitzgerald swiftly gathered them, slipping them into a drawer.

The room, adorned with antique furniture and subtle hints of lavender, spoke of a timeless sophistication. Seated, they delved into a discussion about the potential collaboration between Asante and the gallery, their conversation echoing through the well-appointed room like a symphony of possibilities.

The meeting unfolded seamlessly, the air filled with a shared sense of purpose. The ideas resonated with the gallery owner, and the potential collaboration sparkled with promise. Mrs. Fitzgerald, with a gracious nod, expressed her enthusiasm for the innovative partnership. With the meeting drawing to a close, they decided to reconvene to review the detailed notes taken during their discussion and to finalize the terms of the collaboration. As they bid their farewells, the prospect of a formal contract lingered in the air, a tangible testament to the exciting venture that awaited them.

"Thank you for meeting with us, Mrs. Fitzgerald. I look forward
to working with you." Asante and LaShawn left the office feeling like
something was off.

They walked in silence until they were out of the gallery. On the
sidewalk, they sat on a bench. LaShawn couldn't contain their curiosity
any longer. "You saw something, Asante. What was it?"

Asante couldn't hide her excitement. "I'm so glad to be out of there.
I'm bursting to tell you. You won't believe it. Carved into the corners at
the back of the frame are 'Harriet' and 'Elizabeth'—Hattie and Bessie,"
she said excitedly.

LaShawn was stunned by this revelation. "So, there's a definite
connection. And while you were inspecting the frame, I discreetly
glanced at Mrs. Fitzgerald's desk. Before she shoved all the papers into
the desk drawer, I saw a piece of mail with red lettering. She tried to hide
it, but I could still make out the words 'BANKRUPTCY NOTICE'.
The gallery is in financial trouble. What if the painting wasn't stolen?
What if it was hidden somewhere to claim the insurance money to get
the gallery solvent?"

Asante considered the possibility. "It's a plausible theory. I was
wondering why we were able to get an appointment on such short notice
and there weren't many patrons. Should we take this information to
Officer Jenkins, despite his reservations about our sleuthing in the past?"

LaShawn nodded. "We have to. We have evidence now. There's a
clear connection between the pattern book and Kofi, and no other
artworks in the gallery were stolen, nor were there signs of a break-in.
Add to that the substantial insurance on the painting and the gallery's
financial woes that the insurance payout could resolve, and it's a
compelling case."

"Ok, let's go now."

They proceeded down the street to the police station, the air crisp,
their conversation a dance of speculation and intrigue. They couldn't

shake the feeling that they were tugging at a thread that might unravel
tapestry of secrets binding Bessie's pattern to the painting.

Asante couldn't contain her excitement. "This could be
breakthrough. A connection we've been searching for."

LaShawn nodded, their eyes sparkling with curiosity. "Absolutely.
agree. It's like we're following a thread that leads us closer to unravelin
the mysteries surrounding the pattern book and the stolen artwork."

At the station, the front desk officer, a petite woman with a nam
tag that read 'LAINE', led Asante and LaShawn to Officer Jenkins' smal
office.

"Sarge, these folks here said they have some information about th
gallery heist and that there might be a connection with old Miss Bessi
Washington." Without waiting for a response, she turned to leave, he
gaze traveling the length of the pair. Her dark eyes narrowed witl
suspicion and lingered on each. It was evident that a veil of distrus
shrouded her perception. The weight of her skepticism hung palpably ir
the space long after she was gone, casting a shadow over the forthcomin;
exchange with Officer Jenkins.

Officer Jenkins leaned back in his creaking chair, arms crossed ove
his wide chest, regarding Asante and LaShawn with measured doubt tha
hung in the air. "You both think there's a connection between this Bessi
Washington and the stolen painting? Art and knitting patterns, huh?'
he said, a hint of amusement in his voice.

Asante spoke earnestly, her gaze unwavering. "Officer Jenkins, w
know it sounds unusual, but there's something about it—a thread, ;
connection that we can't ignore. It's as if Bessie's creativity transcend:
time and medium."

LaShawn chimed in, their tone determined. "We're not chasin;
whimsy, Officer. We've done the research. We believe there's a rea
mystery here, waiting to be unraveled."

As they laid out the evidence gleaned from journals and loca
accounts, emphasizing their conviction regarding the connectior

between Bessie Washington and the stolen painting, Officer Jenkins raised an eyebrow. His hesitation lingered, yet he leaned in, absorbing their words with an unexpected attentiveness. The hint of amusement in his eyes softened.

"Well, I've encountered my fair share of peculiar cases in this town, but this one truly stands out. I'll concede, you both possess a knack for rendering even the most fantastical tales strangely plausible." Cautioning against losing themselves in the threads of fantasy, he assured them he would investigate their claims, though making no concrete promises.

A sudden phone call interrupted the room. "This is Office Jenkins," he said with a gruff tone. His stern demeanor faltered for a moment, replaced by a fleeting expression of concern. "Yes, of course," he muttered and hung up. Without divulging details, he excused himself, promising to look into their claims. The silence that followed left them wondering about the unexpected interruption and what secrets it might conceal.

"I wonder what that was all about."

"I don't know but I bet it has something to do with this heist," Asante said.

The sun dipped below the horizon as Asante and LaShawn left the police station, their determination wavered. The fading sunlight bathed the town in a warm, amber glow, casting long shadows across their path. Asante glanced at LaShawn and smiled. "Well, that is more than I'd hoped for. We may not have convinced Officer Jenkins completely, but we're onto something, I can feel it."

LaShawn returned the smile, their eyes sparkling with excitement. "I couldn't agree more, Asante. Our journey has only just begun, and there are more threads to unravel in this tapestry of art and mystery. So, what's our next move, Asante? How do we crack the painting theft and Bessie's mystery?"

Asante pondered for a moment, her expression thoughtful. "I think we should delve deeper into Bessie's life. Maybe visit her old haunts or talk to those who knew her and attended her knitting circles. And we must continue our research on Kofi and his "Child Wearing Blue Mittens with White Snowflakes" series. There might be more clues waiting to be uncovered."

LaShawn nodded in agreement, their determination matching Asante's. "Sounds like a plan. Let's uncover the mysteries that tie Bessie, Kofi, and the stolen painting together, piece by piece."

Just as they were about to turn a familiar corner, LaShawn's sharp eyes caught something unusual—a weathered poster clinging to a light pole.

Staring at the old and faded poster, LaShawn's face went ashen, a mix of surprise and fear dancing in their eyes. Asante, intrigued, followed their gaze. There, on the weathered paper, was an image of a white snowflake on blue, accompanied by elegant calligraphy that read 'knitting circle meeting.'

Gasps escaped them in unison as both remembered the diary entry mentioning knitting meetings Bessie held at her house that people thought were magical. They examined the poster looking for information about the meeting. Has it already happened? The poster held no indication of time or place, leaving them with a cryptic clue. Asante, flipping the paper over with curious hands, searched for any hidden details. The absence of contact information only deepened the mystery, but it was clear—it had to be a clue.

"What could this mean?" Asante wondered aloud, her fingers tracing the edges of the mysterious poster.

LaShawn, equally perplexed, suggested, "Maybe if we visit Mrs. Anderson at the yarn store, she might know something."

Glancing at the time on her phone, Asante urged, "Let's go. The shop is still open but they will close soon.

With a shared sense of urgency, they resumed their journey, the revelation of the enigmatic poster injecting a new layer of intrigue into their quest. The streets whispered with the promise of hidden secrets and

untold stories, the next chapter of their adventure unfolding with each
step.

Chapter 7: Family

Asante and LaShawn burst into The Woolen Oasis, a bit out of breath. The bell above the door jingled merrily as they entered, immediately embraced by the familiar scent of wool and the snug warmth that wrapped around Mrs. Anderson's cozy domain.

"Good evening, dears! What's got you two sprinting back to my humble haven at this time?" Mrs. Anderson greeted them with a warm smile, her eyes sparkling with genuine curiosity.

LaShawn hesitated, glancing at Asante before speaking, "We found this poster about a knitting circle meeting. Do you know anything about it? We think it might be connected to Bessie and the stolen painting."

Mrs. Anderson's eyes widened with recognition as she examined the poster. "Ah, the knitting circle! That's an old tradition in this town. Bessie used to host those magical gatherings. People believed they held the key to her extraordinary creations. Haven't seen a poster for one of those in years. I thought they had faded into memory."

Asante leaned in, a spark of hope in her eyes. "Do you know if this meeting has already happened, or is it upcoming?"

Mrs. Anderson squinted at the poster, deep in thought. "It doesn't say, but if memory serves me right, the meetings usually happened around this time of year. If you're interested, I can share what I know about those gatherings and maybe point you in the right direction."

Asante and LaShawn exchanged determined glances and nodded in unison. "We're very interested, Mrs. Anderson. Any information you can provide might be crucial to unraveling the mystery."

Mrs. Anderson beckoned them to the cozy seating area near the window, where skeins of yarn in a myriad of colors hung like vibrant tapestries. "Take a seat, my dears, and I'll tell you all I know about those enchanting knitting circle meetings from stories I heard from my mother and town's folks when I was growing up."

As they settled into the plush chairs, Mrs. Anderson began to weave a tale of the town's long-standing tradition—the mysterious knitting circle meetings hosted by none other than Bessie Washington.

The tales seemed to dance on the edge of reality and magic. "Bessie's knitting circle meetings were legendary. Held in the heart of autumn, when the leaves whispered secrets and the air crackled with possibility, they were more than just gatherings of folks with needles and yarn. They were a conduit for something otherworldly, an exchange of creativity and energy that left everyone who attended with a sense of wonder."

"Those knitting circles were something special," Mrs. Anderson continued, her eyes reflecting the nostalgia of days gone by. "Bessie would open her home to fellow enthusiasts, and there was an air of magic surrounding those gatherings. Some believed it was where she drew inspiration for her intricate patterns, weaving threads of the mystical into her creations."

LaShawn and Asante listened intently, the yarn store's warm ambiance creating a cocoon around them. Mrs. Anderson continued, "Bessie believed that knitting wasn't just a craft; it was a way to tap into the unseen, to weave a connection between the mundane and the mystical. Those who attended her gatherings spoke of heightened creativity, of visions and dreams that seemed to spill into their waking hours. Picture this: Bessie, surrounded by a circle of eager knitters, each one weaving their own unique pattern. It wasn't just about the stitches; it was about channeling a collective energy, a shared creativity that ranscended the mundane. And in those moments, it's said that something magical happened."

Asante leaned forward, eyes sparkled with fascination, captivated by the unfolding story. "Do you think there's a connection between the knitting circle and the stolen painting?"

Mrs. Anderson was quiet for a moment, then her voice dropped to a conspiratorial tone. "Some believed that the patterns created during those meetings held a special power, a power that transcended the yarn and needles. Bessie, with her unmatched skill, could have inadvertently woven something extraordinary into her creations. As for the stolen painting, I wouldn't be surprised if it carried a piece of that magic within it."

"Why would someone steal a painting for its mystical properties?" LaShawn asked, not expecting an answer.

Mrs. Anderson sighed, her gaze distant for a moment. "Why? The allure of the unknown, dear. Some believe that possessing such a painting grants access to the hidden realms Bessie tapped into. It's a dangerous pursuit, for the line between creativity and chaos is thin. Do I think there's a connection? Absolutely. You see, the magic of those knitting circles wasn't confined to the yarn and needles. Bessie believed that creativity had a life of its own, one that could transcend decades and mediums. The patterns they created held a unique energy, a resonance that echoed through time."

LaShawn's mind whirred with possibilities. "But how does that explain the stolen painting? Can creativity really bridge the gap between knitting and painting?"

Mrs. Anderson nodded knowingly. "Think of it this way: Bessie's knitting patterns weren't just designs; they were a language of their own. A language that spoke to the essence of creativity, a universal force that could be channeled into any form. Her patterns, infused with the collective energy of those knitting circles, could have imprinted something profound onto the stolen painting."

Asante chimed in, "So, the magic isn't in the canvas; it's in the essence of creation itself, a force that can be harnessed by those attuned to its frequency."

Mrs. Anderson smiled, appreciating their grasp of the concept. "Exactly. The stolen painting, carrying the imprint of Bessie's unique creative energy, becomes a vessel for that magic. It's a bridge between the tangible and the intangible, knitting and painting, past and present."

As the conversation unfolded, Mrs. Anderson painted a vivid picture of Bessie's knitting circle, weaving tales that sent shivers down their spines. In the narrative, an elusive figure emerged—Mrs. Ryan. Living in seclusion in a dilapidated house on the outskirts of town, she had become somewhat of a mystery, her presence seldom witnessed for quite some time. Rumors circulated, attributing to her possessed knowledge of the occult and a keen interest in the intersection of art and mysticism.

LaShawn and Asante thanked Mrs. Anderson for her valuable insights, feeling a renewed sense of purpose. The trail of clues was leading them to the heart of the mystery, to the hidden stories intertwined with Bessie's legacy.

With newfound leads, Asante and LaShawn left The Woolen Oasis, their minds buzzing with intrigue. The journey to uncover the secrets of the stolen painting and Bessie's knitting circle had taken an unexpected turn, leading them deeper into the mystical undercurrents of the town's hidden history.

It was late, and the night air held a crisp chill as they made plans to visit the address Mrs. Anderson had discreetly shared—a hidden spot known to be associated with Mrs. Ryan.

The next day, Asante and LaShawn stood in front of the weathered house that belonged to the elusive Mrs. Ryan. The air felt charged with anticipation as they approached the door, their knuckles rapping against the aged wood. After a moment that seemed to stretch into eternity, the door creaked open, revealing a dimly lit interior.

Mrs. Ryan, a wizened figure with piercing eyes that seemed to hold the weight of centuries, regarded them with a mixture of curiosity and suspicion. "What brings you to my doorstep?" Her voice, like rustling leaves, carried an otherworldly quality.

Asante took a deep breath, exchanging a determined look with LaShawn. "We're investigating the stolen painting from the art gallery, and we heard you might have information about Bessie's knitting circle."

A sly smile tugged at the corners of Mrs. Ryan's lips. "Ah, the knitting circle. Bessie's legacy, woven into the very fabric of this town. Come, sit." She gestured for them to enter and toward a table cluttered with ancient tomes, yarn, and peculiar artifacts in a dark and dingy living room.

As they settled, Mrs. Ryan began to unravel the intricacies of Bessie's connection to the mystical arts. "Bessie was a weaver of dreams and realities. Her knitting circles weren't just about yarn and patterns; they were a conduit for the energies that shape our world. She believed in the power of creation, in the threads that connect the seen and the unseen."

LaShawn leaned forward, captivated by Mrs. Ryan's words. "What about the stolen painting? Is it connected to the knitting circle?"

Mrs. Ryan nodded sagely. "Indeed. That painting holds the echoes of those long-forgotten gatherings. Bessie, with her extraordinary talents, wove more than just patterns; she wove spells into her creations. The stolen painting is a vessel, a reservoir of the magical energy that surged through those who participated in the knitting circles."

Asante's mind raced, connecting the dots. "But who would steal it, and why?"

Mrs. Ryan's gaze turned distant. "The allure of power, my dears. There are those who seek to harness the energies of creativity for their own purposes. The stolen painting is a key, a bridge between worlds. In the wrong hands, it could tip the delicate balance between creation and chaos."

LaShawn frowned. "What do we do, then? How do we stop this?"

Mrs. Ryan leaned in, her eyes narrowing with intensity. "You must follow the threads of destiny. Bessie's legacy is not lost; it lives on in the patterns she created. Seek the heart of the painting, and you'll find the answers you seek. But beware, for dark forces may be at play. Trust in your bond, for the strength of family is a powerful thread that can withstand even the most tangled mysteries. Find the last time capsule the town made. It's in the archives. Inside you'll find what Bessie chose to preserve from her past for the future well after her passing."

Armed with fresh knowledge, Asante and LaShawn left Mrs. Ryan's abode, the weight of responsibility settling on their shoulders. The stolen painting was not just a piece of art; it was a conduit to a world where magic and creativity intertwined. The journey ahead promised revelations that could reshape their understanding of Bessie's legacy and the town's hidden history.

Asante and LaShawn left Mrs. Ryan's with a sense of urgency. The streets seemed to murmur secrets, guiding them back to the heart of the town—the archives. Determined, they entered the dimly lit room filled with the hushed rustle of old papers and the musty scent of history.

Asante scanned the shelves exactly where the archivist told them the capsules were saved until her eyes settled on a dusty box tucked away in a corner. "This could be it," she whispered, pulling it out with care.

As they opened the box, a gust of time-stirred air greeted them. Inside, among the relics of the past, lay an assortment of old photos, trinkets, and memories cherished by the town's people. LaShawn's fingers traced the edges of a black and white photograph depicting an older woman with a young girl, both adorned in hand-knit shawls.

Asante peered closer, her eyes widening with recognition. "Hattie and Bessie," she murmured, reading the fragile ink inscription on the back of the photo.

LaShawn pointed to an envelope clipped to the picture. "Look at this."

Carefully, Asante opened the envelope, revealing a delicate piece of lace knitting nestled within. A cryptic note accompanied it, its words a whispered mystery. "Family bond transcends the threads of time."

LaShawn studied the lace, her fingers tracing the intricate patterns. This must be one of Bessie's creations. But what's the connection to the stolen painting?"

Asante's gaze sharpened with realization. "Family bond...could it be the key to unlocking the magic in Bessie's work? Perhaps there's a hidden message in the lace, a pattern that connects the stolen painting to the town's history."

Determined to unravel the mystery, they rushed back to The Woolen Oasis, where Mrs. Anderson awaited with her wealth of knowledge.

As they entered, the bell chimed, and Mrs. Anderson looked up from behind the counter. "Back so soon, my dears? Did Mrs. Ryan shed light on the path you tread?"

Asante held up the lace and the cryptic note. "We found this in the town's archives. It belonged to Bessie. Do you recognize the pattern, or does the note make any sense to you?"

Mrs. Anderson's eyes sparkled with recognition as she took the lace into her hands. "Ah, the intricacies of family bonds and the threads that bind us. This lace carries the essence of Bessie's creations, a language only those attuned to her legacy can decipher. I see that you also have the time capsule?"

LaShawn, so focused on the photo and the lace, forgot that they had the time capsule too. "Yes. There's so much history in there, but we haven't looked beyond what Bessie added."

Asante leaned in, her voice eager. "Can you help us understand? We need to unlock the connection between this lace and the stolen painting."

Mrs. Anderson nodded, a knowing smile playing on her lips. "The lace holds the key to Bessie's secret language. Each pattern tells a story, and when woven together, they reveal the tapestry of the town's hidden history. Let me show you."

Mrs. Anderson took charge and led the pair to the table in the back of the store. Her eyes glinted with a mix of curiosity and determination. "Let's unravel this mystery, shall we?" She carefully laid out the contents of the time capsule on the counter, the delicate lace and the black-and-white photo of Hattie and Bessie drawing everyone's attention.

LaShawn studied the photo, their eyes narrowing in thought. "They look so connected, like there's a story untold."

Mrs. Anderson nodded. "There often is, my dear. Now, let's see what else we have here." She picked up the lace, examining its intricate pattern. "This lace holds secrets, passed down through generations. It's not just a piece of fabric; it's a conduit for something deeper."

"What about the note, Mrs. Anderson? It mentioned something about family bonds."

Mrs. Anderson produced the note, its edges fragile with age. "Family bonds can transcend time, and in this town, they sometimes come with a touch of magic." She pointed to the stitch pattern scratched on the inside of the capsule. "Look closely. This is no ordinary pattern. It's a message from Bessie herself, a code that connects the past to the present."

LaShawn leaned in, their eyes tracing the pattern. "But how does it connect to Kofi? And why use the lace as a conduit?"

Mrs. Anderson smiled knowingly. "Bessie believed in the power of creation, not just as an act but as a bond between family. This lace was crafted with intention, a symbol of the unbroken thread that ties generations together. And see these unique stitches? They hold a hidden message, a message meant for Kofi."

Asante, despite her worries, felt a spark of intrigue. "What's the message, Mrs. Anderson?"

Mrs. Anderson began deciphering the stitches, her fingers moving expertly over the lace. "It's a message of guidance and protection, a legacy passed down through the fabric itself. Bessie, knowing the threads of time and space, wove this message for Kofi, foreseeing a moment when it would be needed the most."

LaShawn, caught between skepticism and fascination, asked, "You're saying Bessie communicated through this lace across decades?"

Mrs. Anderson nodded. "Magic is often woven into the fabric of our lives, and Bessie had a way of threading it into every creation. This lace isn't just a piece of fabric; it's a bridge between generations, a way for Bessie to guide and protect her family, even from beyond. Many of the same stitches used in this lace fabric are used in the scarf that you made Asante, and the socks you are both knitting on right now. The stitches used are deliberate."

As they absorbed the revelation, Mrs. Anderson carefully refolded the lace, placing it back into the capsule. "Take this with you, my dears. It holds the wisdom of generations, and now, it's a part of your journey. The stolen painting, the knitting circle, and Bessie's legacy—they're all interconnected."

Asante, still processing the mystical revelation, clutched the time capsule. "Thank you, Mrs. Anderson. We'll make sense of this, for Bessie, for Kofi, and for our family."

With the weight of the lace-infused message in their hands, Asante and LaShawn left The Woolen Oasis, their resolve renewed. The mysteries surrounding Bessie's legacy were deepening, and the threads of the past were weaving a narrative that connected them to something far beyond their imagination.

Chapter 8: Healing

Asante and LaShawn returned the time capsule back to the shelf as promised. Asante felt an unexplained chill in the air. A subtle shift in the atmosphere that whispered of impending change. The musty and drafty archives now held a faint undercurrent of unease. LaShawn, too, noticed the change, exchanging a glance with Asante that conveyed a shared sense of disquiet.

As they hovered near the diaries and newspaper articles, anticipation hung in the air, making the room feel almost alive, as if an unspoken tension had gripped them both.

As if on cue Asante's phone rang, shattering the delicate balance in the room. She hesitated for a moment before answering, an unspoken fear flickering in her eyes. The call that followed would unravel more than just the mysteries they sought, leaving them with a weight that transcended the stolen painting and Bessie's legacy.

Asante's phone buzzed with Aaliyah's incoming call, and a spark of excitement lit up her eyes. "It's Aaliyah," she said, eagerly grabbing her phone, anticipating a cheerful exchange with her sister.

"Hey, Sis. I'm so glad you called. I was going to call you tonight to tell you all we've discovered, but I can tell you now," she was so excited, she was bouncing on her toes.

The initial joy, however, morphed into confusion as she heard the tremor in Aaliyah's voice on the other end.

"Asante. I have bad news. It's Dad. Come now, he had a heart attack and is in the hospital."

Aaliyah's words hit Asante like a sudden gust of cold wind. Confusion deepened into shock, a heavy realization settling in. A knot tightened in Asante's stomach, a physical manifestation of the emotional storm swirling within. Her breath caught, a brief gasp escaping her lips, as she grappled with the gravity of the news.

In that moment, the familiar archives seemed to fade away and the world around Asante blurred. The call from Aaliyah became a lifeline tethering her to a stark reality—one where the mysteries of stolen paintings and family legacies took a back seat to the urgent pulse of life's unpredictability.

Her knees buckled. She didn't even feel LaShawn holding her up. In a daze she said, "I'll be there right away," and hung up.

"It's my dad. I have to go. I have to go, right now," she stammered, confused. With tears streaming down her face, she couldn't see. She just knew she had to go.

"Whoa, hold on a second. You're in no position to drive like this. Let me take you," LaShawn declared. Drying her eyes with their thumb, they added, "I got you!"

At the hospital, the sterile scent overwhelmed Asante as she rushed through the sliding doors, LaShawn right beside her. The harsh fluorescent lights of the hospital corridor flickered overhead, casting a cold, clinical glow. Asante's heart pounded in her chest, each step echoing a mix of fear and urgency.

As Asante rushed towards ICU, the weight of her father's critical condition was accompanied by the burden of unresolved tensions that lingered between them. The discord stemmed from a profound disagreement, a clash of generations and aspirations. Asante had chosen to abandon the well-trodden path of generations of lawyers in her family, dropping out of Law School during her final year, opting instead to spend a year traveling the globe pursuing her passion for art. The decision

o drop out of law school had sparked a heated argument with her father,
traditionalist who viewed the legal profession as an integral part of
heir family legacy. Asante's success in the art world was a testament to
er talent and determination, but it cast a shadow over her relationship
with her father, creating a gulf that now seemed insurmountable in the
ace of the impending crisis. The hospital corridor echoed with both the
rgency of the present and the echoes of a past disagreement that begged
or resolution.

The ICU waiting room felt suffocating, filled with the low hum of
ushed conversations and the occasional beep of medical equipment.
Asante spotted her family gathered, their faces etched with worry.
Aaliyah rushed to Asante, enveloping her in a tight hug.

"Oh, Asante, I'm so sorry," Aaliyah whispered, her voice choked with
motion.

Asante's gaze darted to her father's room, separated by a thin curtain.
His figure lay still, connected to an array of monitors. The rhythmic
beeping of the machines was both a comfort and a reminder of the
fragility of life.

LaShawn, respectful of the family dynamics, hovered in the
background offering silent support. Asante nodded to LaShawn,
acknowledging the unspoken understanding.

Asante approached her father's bedside, a whirlwind of emotions
clouding her mind. She took a deep breath, summoning the strength to
confront the reality before her.

"Dad," she whispered, her voice trembling. "I'm here."

Her father's eyes fluttered open, a weak smile tugging at the corners
of his lips. "Asante, my dear. I didn't mean to worry you."

Tears welled in Asante's eyes as she grasped her father's frail hand.
Don't worry about that now, Dad. We're here for you."

The room felt heavy with unspoken words. Asante's mind wrestled
with the guilt of their unresolved differences, the echoes of their last
heated argument lingering in the air.

"I'm sorry, Dad. I'm sorry for everything," Asante choked out, he voice breaking.

Her father's gaze softened, and he squeezed her hand gently. "No, m love. I should be the one apologizing. I've been too hard on you."

Asante's tears fell freely as the heaviness of the past seemed to lift, i only for a moment. The beeping of the monitors seemed to synchroniz with the beating of her heart.

"I want you to follow your passion, Asante. Your art, it's a part of you I see that now," her father said, his words carrying a depth of sincerity.

Asante nodded, her heart aching with gratitude and regret. "Dad, love you."

"I love you too, sweetheart. Always have, always will."

The room held a profound silence, broken only by the steady hum o medical equipment. Asante clung to the fleeting moments, her emotion raw and exposed.

In the midst of the hospital's sterile surroundings, the tapestry o family, art, and the mysteries of Bessie's legacy converged. The urgency of life's unpredictability juxtaposed against the backdrop of unresolvec differences and the fragility of time.

As Asante's family gathered around, united in their shared concern the hospital room became a crucible for healing and understanding. The connection between generations, the threads of family woven with love and acceptance, transcended the looming specter of loss.

In that moment, Asante realized that the heart of the mystery wasn' just the stolen painting or the secrets of Bessie's legacy—it was the profound tapestry of family, a narrative still unfolding in the face of life' unpredictable turns.

The hospital room became a sanctuary for reconciliation, where the past and the present intersected, and the fragility of life became a poignant reminder of the bonds that endure.

Chapter 9: Truth

"The socks are finally complete, but why don't I feel more excited?" Asante wondered. It'd been a couple of days since her father's medical incident, and he was recovering nicely at home. Their reconciliation at the hospital felt like the end of the story. Somehow, she expected all the pieces of the mystery to fall into place, but that hadn't happened.

Asante took both completed socks to the kitchen sink, filling it with warm water and grabbing a bottle of wool wash. However, a memory from Bessie's diary made her pause. The story was about a woman abused by her husband whose behavior changed after wearing socks made by Bessie. Asante tried to recall what Bessie added to the wash and remembered a mention of fresh basil. Bessie wrote about being in her kitchen, looking out the window into the night, just like Asante was, inhaling the fresh and cleansing smell of the fresh basil on her sill.

"Could it be? Was that the secret she added—fresh basil?" Contemplating the possibility, Asante dropped a couple of basil leaves into the water with the socks. "That makes sense," she mused. "Basil is known to be a natural cleanser and repellent. So, maybe there's something to this as a spiritual, bad vibes repellant that will bring clarity to this mystery."

Pressing the socks into the water, she let them sit for thirty minutes before removing them and then laying them on the bed in her spare bedroom to dry. However, Asante didn't feel any different and dismissed it as a fancy idea, and decided to go to sleep.

In the early hours, Asante woke abruptly, realizing she knew what happened. Checking her phone, it was 4:14 AM. Contemplating whether to call the police or LaShawn, she decided to wait until morning. Heading to the kitchen to start the coffee, she turned on her laptop, ready to put the final pieces of the puzzle together to present to Officer Jenkins.

By daybreak, she was in Officer Jenkins' office with LaShawn. Without hesitation, Asante methodically laid out their discoveries. She painted a vivid picture of the intricate web they had unraveled, connecting Bessie's patterns, Kofi's artistry, and the cryptic etchings on the stolen painting's frame, all while delving into the gritty details of Mrs. Fitzgerald's financial woes and the suspicious insurance policy.

Officer Jenkins listened with unwavering focus, his initial skepticism conceding to the power of the evidence before him; it was too compelling to ignore. As he absorbed the weight of their findings, a resolute determination surged within him, propelling him headlong into an exhaustive investigation that promised to rock the very foundations of the case.

After a thorough investigation, Officer Jenkins confirmed their suspicions. The new, higher-value insurance policy had indeed been secured just a mere week before the theft, raising red flags. Armed with a court-sanctioned warrant, the police searched the gallery. In the dim recesses of the basement, in a hidden room with dust in the shape of a snowflake, concealed behind another painting within an old trunk, they uncovered the supposed stolen painting, deliberately concealed from view.

By midday, the news broke that the painting was found.

Aaliyah hurried to Asante's apartment, eager to unravel the whole story. Bursting through the door, she exclaimed, "Ok, spill it. I've waited long enough. Tell me everything. What happened?" Spotting LaShawn ı the kitchen setting the table, Aaliyah walked over and gave them a ıug. "Good to see you, LaShawn. You were supposed to keep my sister ut of mess," she said without any heat.

"You know I couldn't stop her even if I wanted," LaShawn replied.

"I can hear you two, you know," Asante said, closing the front door ıd walking into the kitchen to the delicious smells of dinner. "Anyway, hope you don't mind, but I ordered dinner from that Jamaican place we ke. With everything going on today, I didn't have time to cook."

"Yes, that's fine. I don't care what we eat. Just start talking."

They sat down, serving themselves from the takeout containers amily-style.

With a deep breath, Asante told the whole story. "Well, you know finished my second sock yesterday afternoon. After a quick dinner, I lecided to wash and block them so I could wear them to the next Sunday Brunch n' Stitch at the yarn store. I'm getting the sink filled with warm vater, and as I was about to add the wool wash, something told me to top. So, there I am standing over the sink, looking out my window into he dark night, and the story from one of Bessie's diaries came flooding ıack. It was the story of the woman who gave her husband a pair of socks, ınd he went from being an abusive man to a loving husband—exactly vhat she needed. Remember, LaShawn?

"So, recalling the diary entry and Bessie's reference to the herbs on ıer windowsill, I thought, maybe she used basil in the wash. I mean, it vouldn't hurt my knitting. So, I plucked a couple of leaves from my basil ›lant on my windowsill and placed them in the water with the socks. Of ourse, nothing happened. No puffs of smoke or anything. I was pretty lisappointed. I don't know what I expected but I expected something o happen. About half an hour later, I finished the blocking process, laid he socks out on the spare bed, and went to sleep. At the crack of dawn, woke up with this clarity. It all made sense. I dreamt what happened. n my dream, I saw Mrs. Fitzgerald getting a notice. It was about the ›ankruptcy, but not the one we saw that day in her office. It must have been the first notice. Then, in my dream, I saw her walking around the room like a wild cat, and then she stopped suddenly as if hit. Pulling out white gloves from her desk, because she often uses them to handle work in the gallery, she walked down the gallery to the Kofi exhibits and cut out one of the paintings from the frame.

"Did you know that the building where the gallery is now used to be an underground for smuggling? LaShawn told me that the first time we met. Which meant there were lots of hiding places. So, in my dream she took the painting to the basement to a secret compartment. When she opened the door, there was white residue or dust that fell on the ground that looked like a snowflake...like the mittens in the pattern and the painting. I did some research to confirm all that and then called LaShawn when it was light out to go with me to the police station. Of course, Officer Jenkins was skeptical as usual, but he said he'd received a call the day LaShawn and I were in his office about the bankruptcy notice the gallery received and that the insurance claim would be enough to cover the amount needed. He was investigating the insurance fraud angle, but without being able to locate the painting, they were stuck. So when I told them about the hidden rooms, they were able to get a search warrant to look for the dust on the ground that looked like snowflakes. They located the missing painting and were able to put it all together." Asante picked up her glass and took a long gulp of her wine.

With stunned eyes, Aaliyah stared at her sister in amazement. "You did all that? I am so proud of you. I knew you could," she said, "both of you," looking at Asante and then LaShawn.

"Hang on, the news is on with the story," Asante said, eyeing the TV in the corner tuned to the local news on mute. She turned up the volume and they all listened.

The shock waves generated by the revelation of art theft and deception reverberated through the art world, sending tremors of disbelief and outrage. Justice was finally served as the stolen painting was recovered, restoring faith in the integrity of the art community. Kofi's visions, once a perplexing enigma, were no longer a mystery; they were the artistic manifestation of messages from Bessie, guiding the present from the past, across the globe.

With their mission accomplished and the art world forever changed, Asante embarked on a new path alongside LaShawn. As they sat together, absorbing the impact of their actions on the broader canvas of the art world, Aaliyah broke the silence.

"I never imagined we'd be part of something like this," she mused, still processing the whirlwind of events.

Asante smiled, a mixture of relief and satisfaction on her face. "Sometimes, you stumble upon mysteries that demand solving. And, well, we just happened to untangle this one."

LaShawn chimed in, "It's incredible how an antique knitting pattern book led us to all of this. Art, mystery, and justice—all intertwined."

Aaliyah looked at Asante, her eyes reflecting admiration. "You've got a knack for unraveling mysteries, Sis. Who knew your knitting skills would become the key to exposing a fraud?"

They shared a moment of laughter, the weight of the recent days lifting as the camaraderie among the three deepened.

Asante turned towards LaShawn, gratitude in her eyes. "None of this would have happened without you. Thank you for being by my side through all of it."

LaShawn shrugged modestly. "Just doing what friends do. And, besides, it was an adventure I wouldn't have missed for anything."

With that, they stood in the glow of the news report, realizing that their actions had left an indelible mark on the art world, connecting the past and present in ways they hadn't anticipated.

As the news segment concluded, the room fell silent. The chapter, filled with twists, turns, and unexpected revelations, had come to an end. But for Asante, LaShawn, and Aaliyah, a new chapter, one forged by friendship, determination, and the unraveling of mysteries, had just begun.

Chapter 10: Epilogue

A month had slipped by since Asante, with LaShawn, unraveled the mystery of the antique knitting pattern book and the daring painting heist. Her father's recovery was a slow and steady process, and the bond between them was healing alongside his health. Time had woven its threads into the fabric of Asante's life, and the lessons she had learned from the pattern book continued to shape her journey.

Asante's friendship with LaShawn had transformed into something more profound. Their love had grown like a well-knit garment, each stitch representing a shared moment, a shared dream, and a shared future. They had become partners, their story a testament to the enduring beauty of love that bloomed amid the threads of knitting and art.

One evening, as they shared a quiet moment on the couch, Asante knitting a hat and LaShawn reading a research journal, Asante couldn't help but marvel at the intricate pattern of their intertwined lives. LaShawn reached over and placed a gentle kiss on Asante's forehead, and they reveled in the warmth of their love, grateful for the journey that had brought them together.

Meanwhile, Asante's father, recovering at home, had taken up knitting as a form of therapy. The rhythmic click of needles filled the house, becoming a soothing soundtrack to their healing bonds. Asante and her father spent many evenings together, exchanging stories and laughter, their connection strengthening with each passing day.

As their lives settled into a comforting rhythm, a mysterious thread of curiosity was about to unravel once more. On a lazy Saturday afternoon, Aaliyah explored a thrift store and stumbled upon a partially finished crochet blanket. Pinned to it was a note that read, "To the one who finds this, continue weaving the threads of mystery. This blanket is meant for someone special."

Intrigued, Aaliyah felt a familiar spark of excitement. She looked at the incomplete masterpiece and, with determination in her eyes, decided to embark on an adventure—a journey to unravel the mystery behind the crochet blanket, its intended recipient, and the story it held within its colorful strands. And so, the threads of mystery continued to weave their enchanting tale, beckoning Aaliyah into the unknown as a new chapter unfolded.

DON'T MISS OUT!

CLICK THE LINK BELOW and sign up to receive email updates from Tian Connaughton when she publishes new books and patterns. There's no charge and no obligation.

tianconnaughton.ck.page/theweeklyyarn[1]

---

1. https://tianconnaughton.ck.page/theweeklyyarn

ABOUT THE AUTHOR

TIAN CONNAUGHTON is a crochet and knitwear designer technical editor, coach, and author. With over a decade of experience working with major brands and world-class designers in the fiber industry, she is on a mission to highlight and amplify the stories of historically underrepresented voices.

Tian lives in rural Western Massachusetts with her husband, son, 4-legged fur babies, and a coop full of hens.

Learn   more   about   Tian   and   her   work   at www.tianconnaughton.com[2].

---

2.   http://www.tianconnaughton.com

ACKNOWLEDGMENTS

I am deeply grateful to the talented individuals whose contributions played an integral role in bringing this novel to life. Their dedication and expertise have enriched the pages of this book, and I am truly thankful for their support.

First and foremost, I extend my heartfelt appreciation to Samantha M. Ryan [Copy Editor], whose attention to detail and keen editorial insights have polished this manuscript to perfection.

A special thank you goes to Madelyn Fischer [Book Cover Designer] for crafting a visually stunning and captivating cover that beautifully captures the essence of the story within.

I would also like to express my gratitude to Kelly Newman [Beta Reader], whose thoughtful feedback and constructive criticism have been instrumental in shaping the narrative.

Thank you all for being an essential part of this creative process and contributing to the realization of this novel.

ALSO BY Tian Connaughton

● Cardigans For Every Body: because every body is worthy

● Unlock Your Inner Designer: How to start designing

● Pattern Launch Plan: Sell more patterns consistently
without being sleazy

tianconnaughton.com/books[3]

PATTERN

PROTECTION SCARF

SKILL LEVEL: ADVANCED Beginner/Intermediate

Yarn: DK weight (approximately 250 yards)

Needle: US size 8 (5 mm), straight or circular

Extras: Yarn needle for weaving in ends; two (2) removable stitch markers; smooth waste yarn and crochet hook for provisional cast on.

Gauge: 18 sts and 24 rows = 4" [10 cm] in Stockinette Stitch

SCARF INSTRUCTION

Using crochet hook and smooth waste yarn, provisional cast on 24 sts.

Row 1 (RS): K4, place marker (pm), k16, pm k4.

From this point, slip marker (sm) as you come to it.

Row 2 (WS): K4, sm, p16, sm, k4.

Row 3: K4, sm, *k2, k2tog, yo; rep from * to marker, sm, k4.

Row 4: Rep Row 2.

Row 5: K all sts.

Row 6: Rep Row 2

Row 7: K4, sm, *k2tog, yo, k2; rep from * to marker, sm, k4

Row 8: K4, sm, p16, sm, k4.

Work these 8 rows for a total of 45 times (360 rows).

ON THE LAST ROW, DO not turn work. Start working the instructions for the Edging, beginning with the Cable Cast On.

FOR THE EDGING AT THE beginning of the scarf (the provisional cast on), remove the provisional cast on and place stitches on needles.

EDGING INSTRUCTION

With yarn, cable cast on 9 sts, turn work.

Row 1: K8, ssk (slip the final st of the edge sts, then slip the next st from the body of the scarf, knit these 2 sts together), turn work.

Row 2: Sl1 pwise, k2, [k2tog, yo] twice, k1, yo, k1, turn work (10 edge sts).

Row 3: K9, ssk (edge st with next body st), turn work.

Row 4: Sl1 pwise, k1, [k2tog, yo] twice, k3, yo, k1, turn work (11 edge sts).

Row 5: K10, ssk (edge st with next body st), turn work.

Row 6: Sl1 pwise, [k2tog, yo] twice, k5, yo, k1, turn work (12 edge sts).

Row 7: K11, ssk (edge st with next body st), turn work.

Row 8: Sl1 pwise, k2, [yo, k2tog] twice, k1, k2tog, yo, k2tog, turn work (11 edge sts).

Row 9: K10, ssk (edge st with next body st), turn work.

Row 10: Sl1 pwise, k3, yo, k2tog, yo, k3tog, yo, k2tog, turn work (10 edge sts).

Row 11: K9, ssk (edge st with next body st), turn work.

Row 12: Sl1 pwise, k4, yo, k3tog, yo, k2tog, turn work (9 edge sts).

Rep Rows 1-12 until all sts along the end of the scarf are worked.

BO all edge sts kwise.

FINISHING

Weave in all ends and block to open up the edge stitch pattern.

FOR THE COMPLETE PATTERN for the Protection Scarf, with list of abbreviations used, charts, tutorials, and options to make the scarf beginner friendly, go to www.tianconnaughton.com/protection-scarf[4]

---

4. http://www.tianconnaughton.com/protection-scarf

Milton Keynes UK
Ingram Content Group UK Ltd.
UKHW022242010524
442049UK00001BA/45

9 798987 617649